The Shabbat Treasure

Evelyn Goldfinger

Illustrations by
Marcelo Gorenman

To Mom and Dad. Thank you for setting our
Shabbat table with the values of family, community,
Holiness, song, joy and the treasures of Judaism. To
F.P. and to J.P.G. and the new generation, for whom
the tradition goes on even more wonderfully.
—E.G.

For my brother, Claudio. He always seems two steps
ahead, and yet I always know he is behind me if I fall.
—M.G.

Copyright © 2018 by Evelyn Goldfinger

Illustrations by Marcelo Gorenman
Graphic Design by Federico Pallas

info@torahtron.com

ISBN: 978-1-7335165-0-1

Printed in the United States of America
First Edition, 2019

www.torahtron.com

Summary:
Eve is getting ready to receive the Shabbat Queen and
needs to make sure everything is perfect. However, Pirate
Leo wants to play and he messes up with her plans.
Together they will discover the true Shabbat treasure.

It was Friday afternoon and Eve could not wait to meet the Shabbat Queen. She excitedly practiced her curtsy bow in front of the mirror. She had never met a queen before.

"Everything must be just perfect to receive the Shabbat Queen," Eve declared as she put her toys away.

Just then, her little brother Leo entered, leaving mud prints on the floor.

"I found a dinosaur egg in the backyard. Join me, Explorer Eve!"

"I can't play now. The Shabbat Queen is coming!

"Who?"

4

Eve explained that every Friday night the Shabbat Queen brings joy, songs and blessings to each home.

And that it is very important to clean up, take a bath and set the Shabbat table with candles, grape juice and Challah. Eve even had her own very special Shabbat dress ready!

"C'mon, Leo, let's clean up!"

That did not sound like fun to Leo. He wanted to play. He insisted: "Let's play Robots! Astronauts! Circus clowns!" But Eve was too busy.
Leo stormed out before Eve could hand him the broom.

5

Eve had just finished wiping the mud off the floor when she heard a loud noise coming from Leo's room.

"I'm the Shabbat Pirate and I took the Shabbat elements. If you want to meet the Shabbat Queen, you need to succeed at my three fun challenges," Leo exclaimed. Eve really needed the candles, the Kiddush cup and the Challah! But where were they? Pirate Leo wanted her to come up with three fun ways to get ready for Shabbat.

"For our first challenge, we'll clean up your room… In a fun way!" Eve added cheerfully, trying to sound convincing.

Eve turned on her cheery music and soon they were arranging the toys by size, sorting the clothes by color and organizing the books alphabetically!

7

"Fun challenge number 1 completed!" declared Pirate Leo, and he opened his treasure chest. Eve took out the candles and as she was reaching for the Challah bread, Leo closed the chest. "Don't forget about fun challenge number 2, Eve. It has to be even more fun!" Leo warned her.

8

Eve looked at the time. Leo still needed to take a bath. She filled the bathtub with so many bubbles that they started to flood the bathroom. Big, small and huge bubbles everywhere! Leo giggled. Before he knew it, he was washing his head, shoulders, knees and toes!

Eve sang and her voice
echoed throughout the room.

"*Take a bath from head to feet*
The Shabbat Queen we will meet.

Take a bath full of bubbles
And you'll wash away all your troubles.

Wash your head
From thoughts that make you sad.
Wash your feelings
Keep them happy in your heart.

Wash your mouth,
Put on a smile from end to end.
Wash your hands and
Let's get ready to help a friend."

10

Leo was having so much fun that he did not want to leave the bathtub!

"Fun challenge number 2 completed!" Pirate Leo declared.

Leo put on clean clothes and Eve changed into her special Shabbat dress. She twirled and twirled thinking about how soon she would meet the Shabbat Queen.

Eve took the Challah bread from the chest and reached for the Kiddush cup. Leo closed the chest.
"Don't forget about fun challenge number 3, Eve. It has to be even more fun than challenges number 1 and 2."

Eve realized that the table wasn't set! She brought out a big and beautiful tablecloth. Eve and Leo played hide and seek with it and then used it as a parachute to go down the stairs.

Next, they sang together as they placed the tablecloth, silverware, plates, napkins and glasses on the table. Eve even showed Leo how to fold the napkins into little pirate ships.

Fun challenge number 3 was completed!

13

Eve headed for the chest trunk and took the
Kiddush Cup. But Leo grabbed the grape juice
and wouldn't let go. He wanted to keep playing.

"The Shabbat Queen will arrive any minute now.
Give me the grape juice, Leo."

"It's PIRATE Leo!
And you can't have it!"
Leo took the grape juice
bottle and ran.

15

Eve followed him rapidly. As Leo ran away, he tripped, dropping the bottle and spilling grape juice all over the floor. Leo hurried and picked up the bottle and cleaned the floor.

Then he saw it: a grape juice stain on Eve's perfect Shabbat dress.

"My dress! It's ruined!" Exclaimed Eve. "Now nothing is perfect for the Shabbat Queen".
Leo thought for a minute. There was no time to wash the stain off. "I'm so sorry, Eve. I didn't mean to ruin your Shabbat."

"It's OK, Leo. But I guess I won't get to meet the Shabbat Queen tonight." A tear escaped Eve's eye.

Leo wanted to help his sister. He found Eve's tiara in her room and handed it to her along with a scepter. "You are our own Shabbat Queen, Eve. Every Shabbat you bring us joy, songs and blessings and that's what the Shabbat Queen does."

18

Eve smiled and put the pirate hat back on Leo's head. He looked at her, confused, and Eve proclaimed: "Even the Shabbat Queen needs a Shabbat Pirate to remind her that welcoming Shabbat is a fun treasure."

19

Shabbat Queen Eve and Shabbat Pirate Leo
said the blessings that Friday evening. They
looked up in the sky and discovered seven
bright stars that were arranged like a carriage.
As they sang together, Eve and Leo could
actually feel the Shabbat Queen arriving.

בָּרוּךְ אַתָּה יי אֱלֹהֵינוּ מֶלֶךְ
הָעוֹלָם אֲשֶׁר קִדְּשָׁנוּ בְּמִצְוֹתָיו
וְצִוָּנוּ לְהַדְלִיק נֵר שֶׁל שַׁבָּת

BARUCH ATA ADONAI, ELOHEINU MELECH
HA-OLAM, ASHER KIDSHANU B'MITZVOTAV
VITZIVANU L'HADLIK NER SHEL SHABBAT.

Blessed are you God, Ruler of the Universe,
who sanctified us with the commandment
of lighting Shabbat candles.

בָּרוּךְ אַתָּה יי
אֱלֹהֵינוּ מֶלֶךְ הָעוֹלָם
בּוֹרֵא פְּרִי הַגָּפֶן

BARUCH ATA ADONAI,
ELOHEINU MELECH HA-OLAM,
BOREH P'RI HAGAFEN.

Blessed are you God, Ruler of the Universe,
who creates the fruit of the vine.

בָּרוּךְ אַתָּה יי
אֱלֹהֵינוּ מֶלֶךְ הָעוֹלָם
הַמוֹצִיא לֶחֶם מִן הָאָרֶץ

BARUCH ATA ADONAI,
ELOHEINU MELECH HA-OLAM,
HAMOTZI LECHEM MIN HA'ARETZ.

Blessed are you God, Ruler of the Universe,
who has brought forth bread from the earth.

Shalom, Shabbat! Shabbat Shalom!

Torahtron

Jewish Educational Theater

Check out the stage show
The Shabbat Treasure
by Evelyn Goldfinger
at www.torahtron.com

Made in the USA
Columbia, SC
08 May 2022

60137527R00015